For my mother and father
—C.C.

For DK Dyson, my "Spirit Woman," my wife, carrier of sound,
vision, and magic. And for Fletcher Johnson,
Jim Hamilton, Hollis King, and Carlos Santana
for the presence of their spirits in my life.
—R.G.

Spirit Seeker

JOHN COLTRANE'S MUSICAL JOURNEY

by Gary Golio   PAINTINGS BY Rudy Gutierrez

Clarion Books | Houghton Mifflin Harcourt | Boston New York 2012

"My music is the spiritual expression of what I am. ... I want to speak to their souls."
—John Coltrane

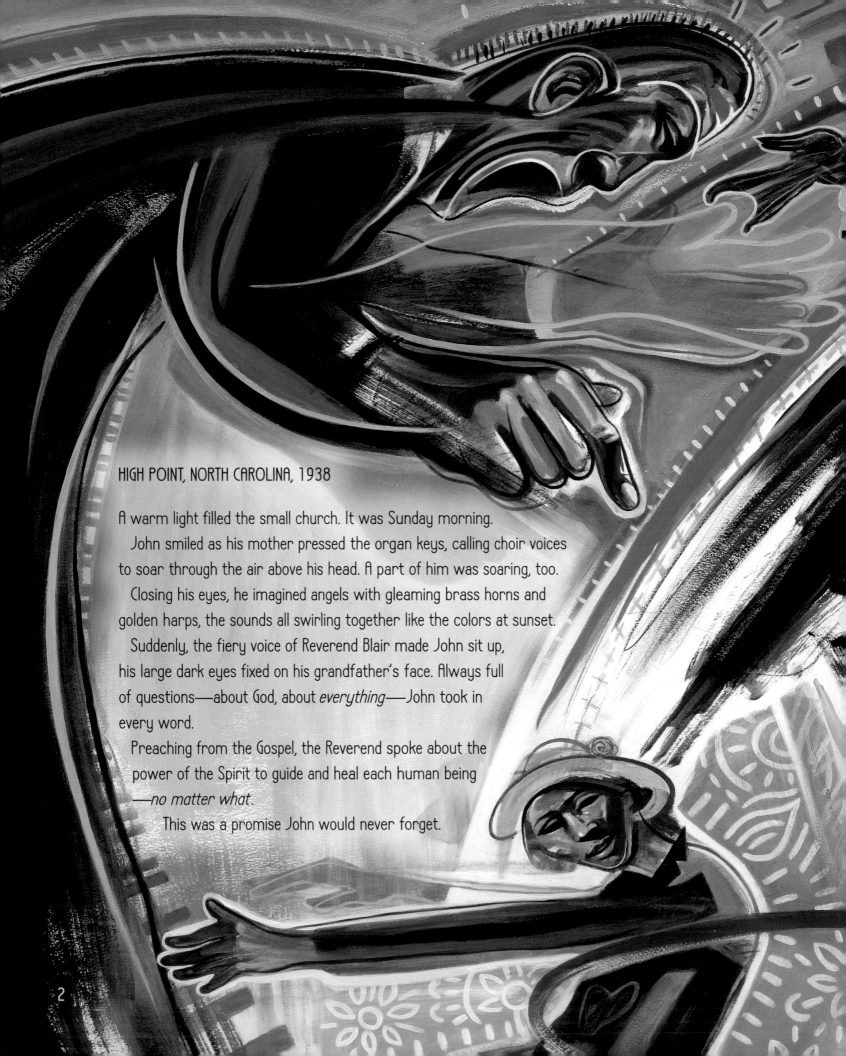

HIGH POINT, NORTH CAROLINA, 1938

A warm light filled the small church. It was Sunday morning.

John smiled as his mother pressed the organ keys, calling choir voices to soar through the air above his head. A part of him was soaring, too.

Closing his eyes, he imagined angels with gleaming brass horns and golden harps, the sounds all swirling together like the colors at sunset.

Suddenly, the fiery voice of Reverend Blair made John sit up, his large dark eyes fixed on his grandfather's face. Always full of questions—about God, about *everything*—John took in every word.

Preaching from the Gospel, the Reverend spoke about the power of the Spirit to guide and heal each human being —*no matter what*.

This was a promise John would never forget.

At twelve years old, John had a very sweet life.
He lived in the Reverend's two-story house
at the top of a hill, with Mama and Papa,
Grandma Blair, Aunt Bettie,
and cousin Mary.

John would roller-skate down the long, paved street with Mary by his side. There were baseball games and hide-and-seek with friends, but also hours for sitting alone and making model planes, cutting and fitting every tiny piece.

At the family feast each week, plates were piled high with fried chicken, hominy grits, corn bread, collards—and John's favorite, sweet potato pie.

Life was like a little slice of heaven.

John's father, J.R., ran his own tailor shop. He'd play the ukulele for friends there after work, singing tender ballads in a deep, soulful voice.

At home, John and Mary liked to sit outside J.R.'s bedroom and listen to him fill the house with songs from his violin.

With eyes like an owl, John watched Papa turn feelings into sound.

Two weeks before Christmas, Reverend Blair died. He was the head of the family, and everyone felt lost without him.

Three weeks later, J.R. died of cancer. Now, the family was in shock.

Mary cried for days, but John was silent. He'd have trouble breathing at night, and sometimes forget what Papa looked like. Thoughts about God, life, and *death* ran through his mind like wildfire, but left him frozen and afraid. He shared his feelings only with Mama.

In a gentle voice, she'd remind him to read his Bible, and to have faith.

That spring, Grandma Blair died. Mary's father, too, would be gone the next year.

It seemed like the sweetness of life had vanished forever.

Left with no money, Mama and Aunt Bettie took jobs at the whites-only country club in town, where John found work shining shoes.

They also rented out the top-floor bedrooms of the house to boarders, and everyone in the family slept downstairs.

11

Missing Papa, John turned to the radio for music. Big bands were all the rage, but there were only a few famous black bandleaders, like Duke Ellington and Count Basie.

One of John's favorite musicians was Lester Young, who played tenor saxophone with the Count. Lester's sound was bouncy but deep, laughter sprinkled with tears.

For John, it was like an echo of Papa's voice.

John started high school just as a black pastor in town was rounding up used instruments for a community band. Lessons were held in the basement of the church.

Beginning on the alto saxophone, John was the first at practice and the last to leave. Back home, he'd sit at the dining room table by himself, running the notes over and over through his old worn horn.

Playing made John come alive. Now *he* was filling the house with sound—mellow love songs or spunky swing music, it didn't matter.

Different songs for different moods. Papa would have understood.

After joining the high school band, John took his horn everywhere. Music made him happy, and it seemed like what he was meant to do with his life.

As he listened to Johnny Hodges—a musician in Duke Ellington's band with a sound soft as velvet—John felt the sax becoming more a part of him. He loved the clicking of the keys, the feel of the mouthpiece between his lips and teeth, the shine of the brass, and the way it sat on his chest, close to his heart.

As he practiced for hours in the music room, his clear, warm notes floated through the school.

Shy and quiet, he let the horn become his voice.

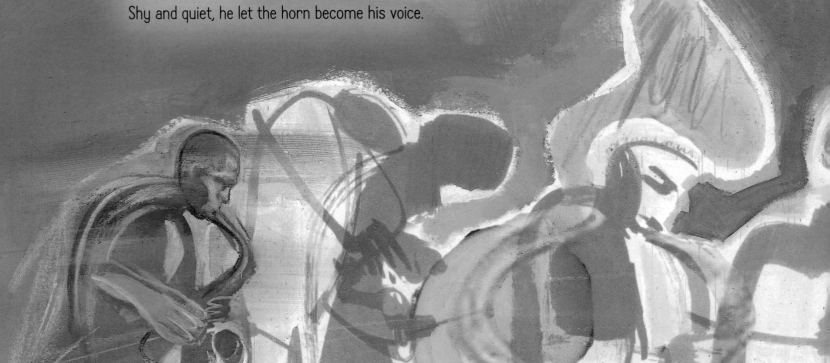

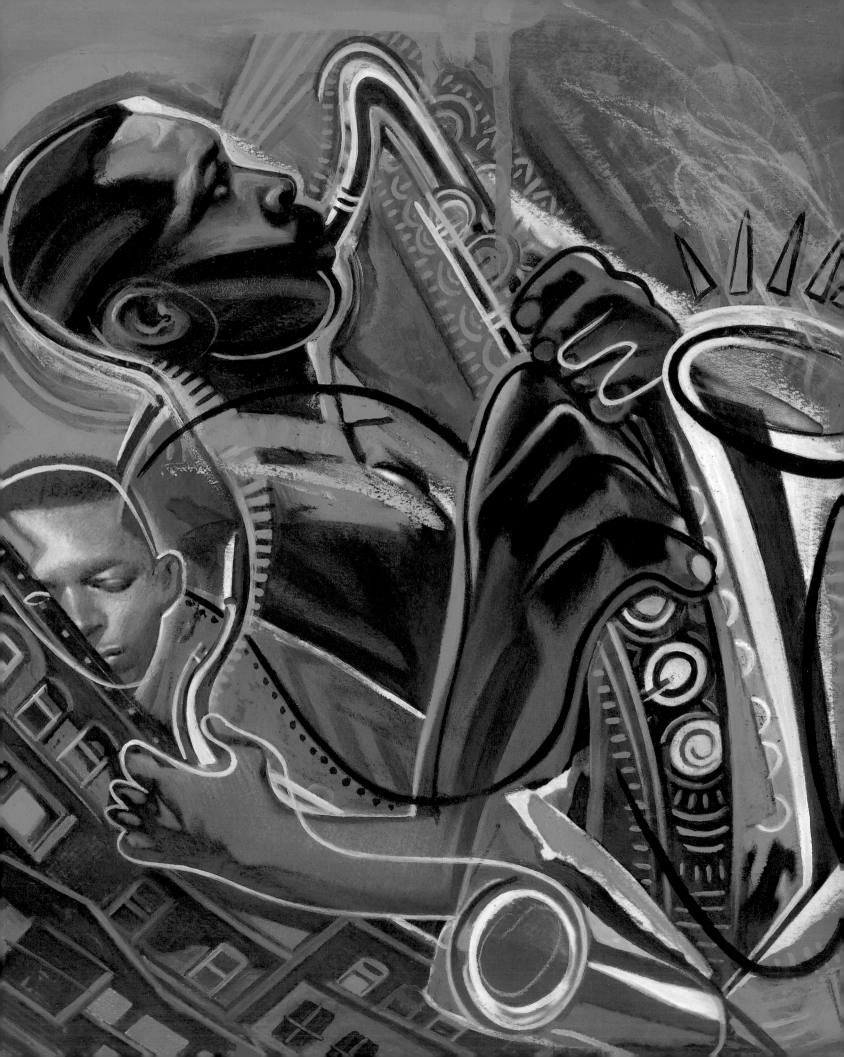

In John's last year of high school, Mama left High Point for a better job up north. A few months later, Mary and Aunt Bettie went to live with relatives, leaving John at home alone.

On a postcard, he wrote to Mary, "I sure wish y'all would come home. I miss you."

Wrapping himself up in music, he practiced constantly. At Friday night parties with friends, he began drinking alcohol to feel less shy—and less lonely.

But the loneliness only grew. John even started to wonder if God really *was* there—watching over him and listening—and he wanted an answer.

Out in the backyard, late one night, he raised his horn to the dark, distant sky. Notes went flying upward, shot at the stars as if to say, *Look, here I am, trying to light my way with this horn!*

But the stars were silent.

After high school John left for Philadelphia, a city brimming with jazz and blues.

Leaving his borrowed instruments behind, he worked at a sugar factory and lived with cousin Mary and Aunt Bettie in a small apartment. When Mama visited one weekend, she bought him a special gift—finally, a saxophone of his own.

Now John reached for the horn first thing in the morning. He began taking classes, studying classical and modern music, always doing more than his teachers asked.

After work he practiced in his room, or in a nearby church, where each note echoed like a small prayer.

Late at night, he'd fall asleep with the saxophone cradled in his arms.

John began playing with big bands and small blues groups. At local clubs and concert halls, he and his friends listened to the hottest musicians in jazz.

That's when he first heard Charlie "Bird" Parker. With quick blasts of notes and long, wild solos on the sax, Bird was creating a bold type of jazz called *bebop*. Filled with jumping beats and playful sounds, it set John's heart racing.

He put Bird's picture on the wall of his room, and tried to catch the man's spirit in his horn.

Like an express train, John was picking up musical styles wherever he went, gaining speed, energy, and rhythm. Friends called him "The Swinging One."

Hired to tour with some well-known bands, he was out on the road for weeks at a time, far from friends and family. Staying in one dark hotel room after another, he found each new city cold and lonely. As a black man, John saw the fear and suspicion in people's eyes when he walked through their towns. The world seemed full of strangers, and empty of friends.

Sad and tired, John soon stopped going to church or reading the Bible. He drank alcohol with other musicians at the clubs and bars where they played. Sometimes he was even told to "walk the bar" with his sax—parading along the top of the counter like a circus performer—and that only made him feel worse.

Now John Coltrane *really* had the blues, and they had him, too.

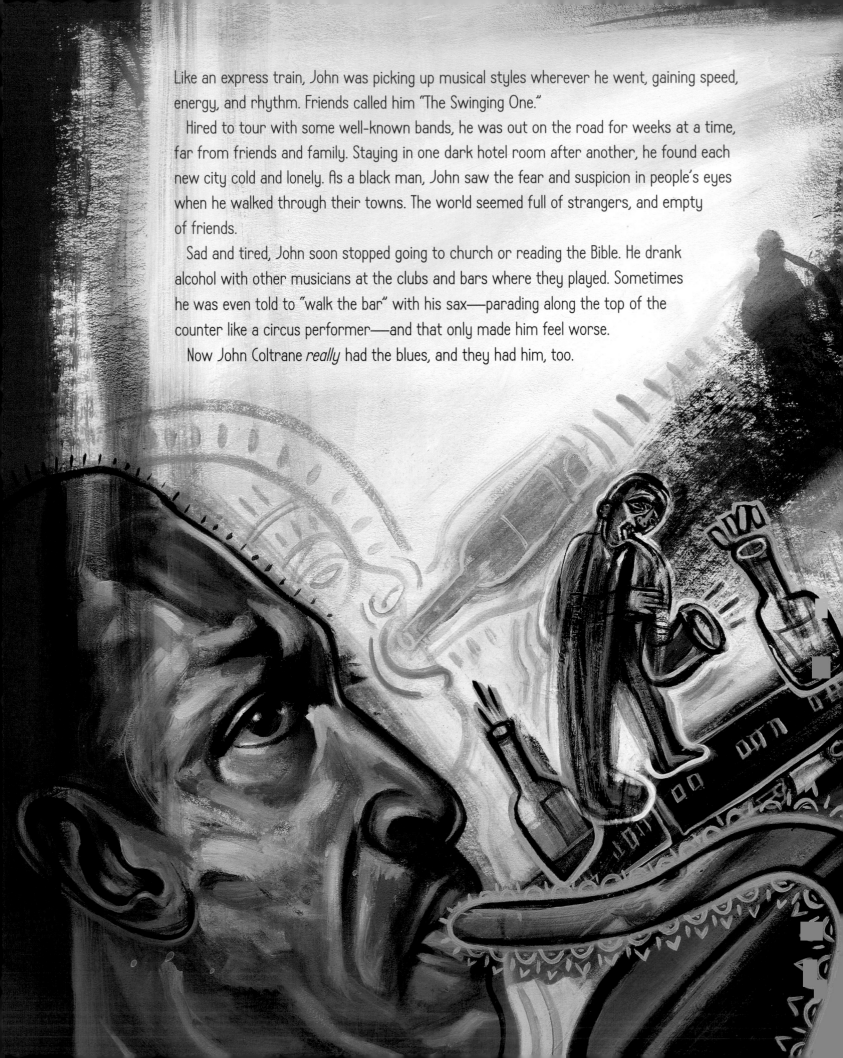

By age twenty-four, John's devoted
playing had earned him respect.
Dizzy Gillespie—the "high priest
of bebop"—and Johnny Hodges,
John's early hero, each asked him
to join their bands for a time.
He was searching, learning,
stretching himself musically,
and these men became his teachers.
Around this time, a friend and fellow musician
lent John some books about
world religions—different ways of
thinking about God and life.
These were *old* beliefs and ideas,
from China, India, Africa,
and Japan, but they were new
to John. One idea was that the
human body is a sacred place—
like a church—that must be kept
clean, open to the light and air.

Reading these books,
John felt as if some sunlight
and fresh air were entering
his own life again. Still, the sadness
he'd known for years hung over him,
dark and heavy, like an overcoat
he couldn't take off. He even tried
using drugs to take away his
painful feelings, to quiet his
thoughts and numb his body.
    But drugs couldn't do that.
And John couldn't stop using them.
    He began falling asleep onstage.
Or showing up late, only to be fired.
    Part of him stood in the darkness,
while another part was searching
            for the light.

Then John met a woman named Naïma. Easy to talk to, she also believed that life, and the body, were sacred. They married, and John felt hopeful again.

When Miles Davis—a brilliant young star of the jazz world—asked John to join his group, it seemed like a fresh start.

His playing became faster, bolder, as he experimented with sound itself. He was pushing the saxophone to sing in new and unusual ways, and Miles gave him the freedom to find his own place in the music.

But Miles wouldn't let John use drugs. He had quit them himself, and told John to do the same.

When John couldn't, he lost his job.

More than that, he had lost his way.

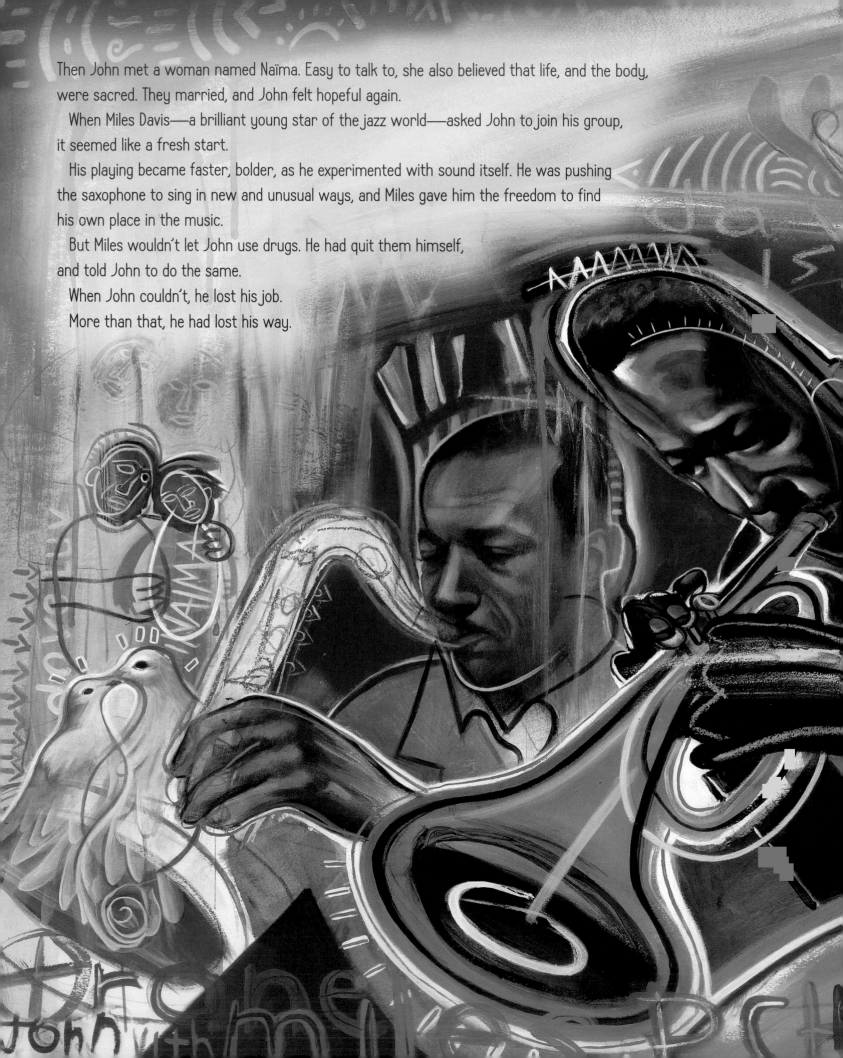

ed garland

23

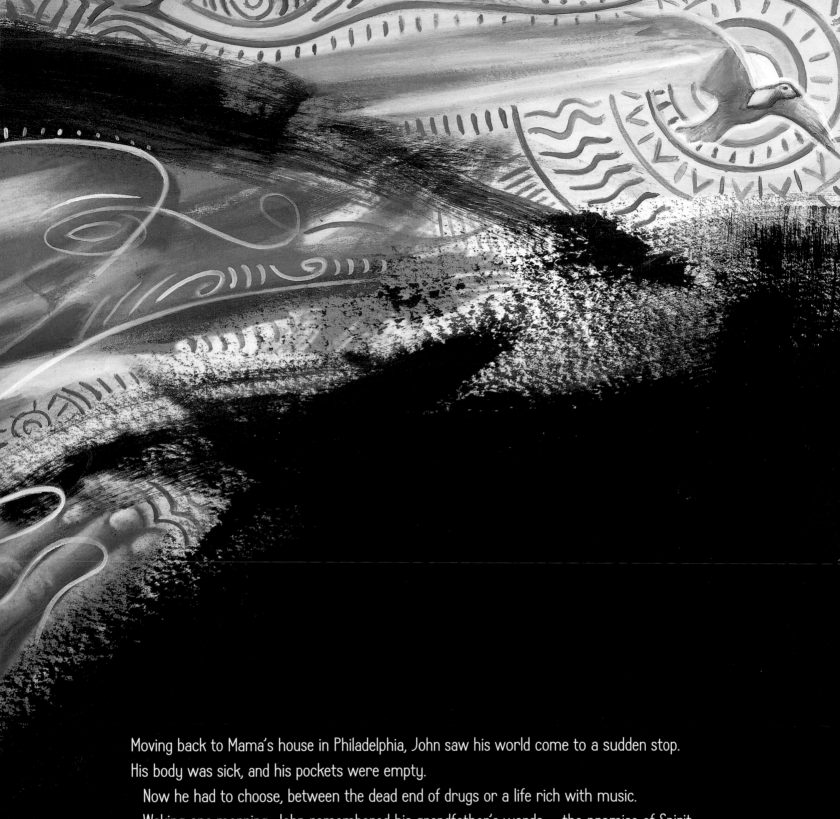

Moving back to Mama's house in Philadelphia, John saw his world come to a sudden stop. His body was sick, and his pockets were empty.

Now he had to choose, between the dead end of drugs or a life rich with music.

Waking one morning, John remembered his grandfather's words—the promise of Spirit, and of healing. He asked Mama and Naïma for help.

With nothing to eat and only water to drink, he stayed alone in his room, resting and praying, as the drugs slowly left his body. It was painful, but John felt that he was being cleansed—made new again.

When he came out, a few days later, he was *free*.

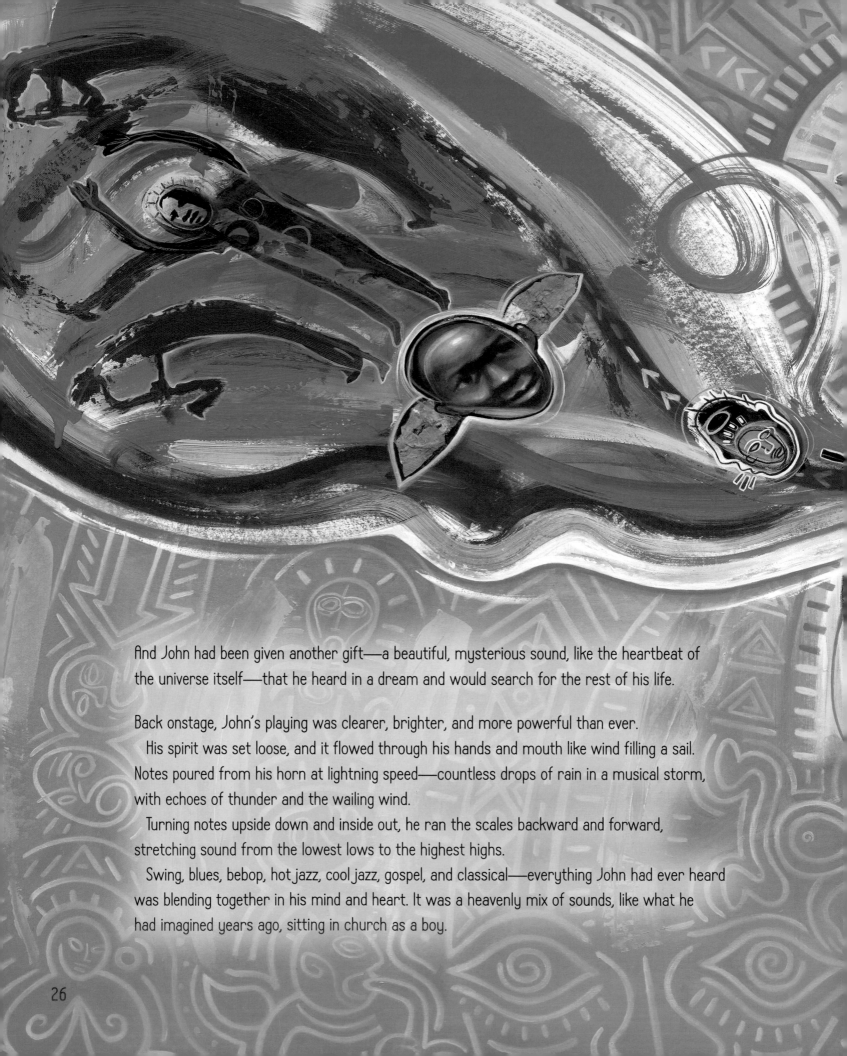

And John had been given another gift—a beautiful, mysterious sound, like the heartbeat of the universe itself—that he heard in a dream and would search for the rest of his life.

Back onstage, John's playing was clearer, brighter, and more powerful than ever.

His spirit was set loose, and it flowed through his hands and mouth like wind filling a sail. Notes poured from his horn at lightning speed—countless drops of rain in a musical storm, with echoes of thunder and the wailing wind.

Turning notes upside down and inside out, he ran the scales backward and forward, stretching sound from the lowest lows to the highest highs.

Swing, blues, bebop, hot jazz, cool jazz, gospel, and classical—everything John had ever heard was blending together in his mind and heart. It was a heavenly mix of sounds, like what he had imagined years ago, sitting in church as a boy.

26

Now musicians and critics packed the clubs,
caught in the spell of his playing.

Rejoining Miles's group, John breathed new life into
his saxophone, feeding it with fresh musical ideas and
finding inspiration everywhere.

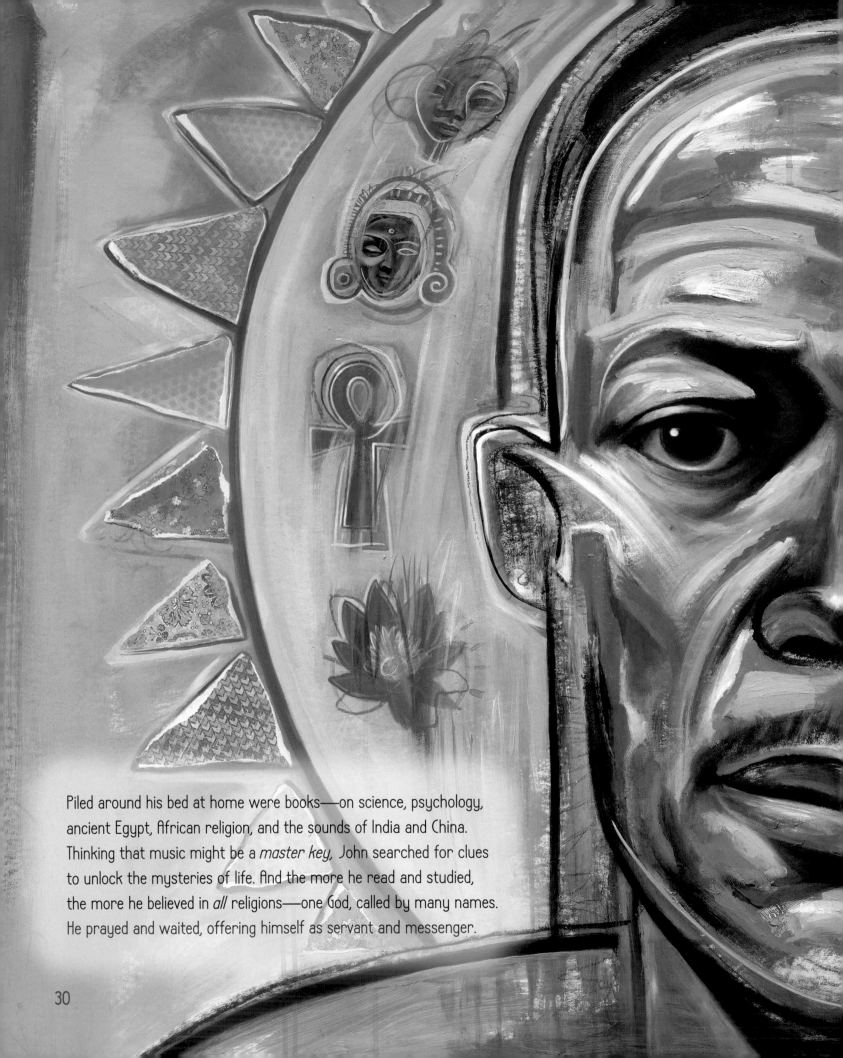

Piled around his bed at home were books—on science, psychology, ancient Egypt, African religion, and the sounds of India and China. Thinking that music might be a *master key,* John searched for clues to unlock the mysteries of life. And the more he read and studied, the more he believed in *all* religions—one God, called by many names. He prayed and waited, offering himself as servant and messenger.

Then, in one big musical leap, John composed the songs for a record called *Giant Steps*. Full of difficult and exciting new pieces, it brought him success, attention, and the chance to lead his own group.

He was finally ready to start preaching with his horn.

Like his grandfather before him, John wanted to wake people up and call them to worship. If music could make people laugh, dance, and sing—even bring them to tears—it could open their hearts and minds and bring them closer to God.

Now, when he played for hours in concerts and clubs, he was like a man in a trance—a holy man, shouting out his love of life to the whole human race.

33

Meditating at home one night, John felt the Spirit take hold of him. Later, he would tell Mama of his vision, and of the music that came to him. It would become the ultimate expression of his spiritual search, a masterpiece, his offering to the Lord. He'd call the work *A Love Supreme*.

Opening with a metal gong that shimmers like a church bell, the album brings the saxophone, piano, bass, and drums together in a musical prayer of praise and thanksgiving. It's as if the instruments are playing hide-and-seek with God and finding Him everywhere—in every sound and note they make.

Through it all, John leads his group of musical explorers with the voice of his horn. Sweet and slow, fiery and fast-moving, his saxophone is at times the roar of a lion, the laughter of a child, a foghorn cutting through the mists . . . the song of the human heart reaching up to heaven.

"There is never an end. There are always new sounds to imagine; new feelings to get at."
—John Coltrane

AFTERWORD

Music and religion were the twin forces that shaped John Coltrane's early years. Both of his grandfathers were Methodist ministers, and each of his parents was a skilled musician.

In North Carolina during the 1930s, the church was the center of black community life. At a time when discrimination was widespread, the church offered comfort, hope, and guidance. One way it did this was through music.

Churches like Reverend Blair's drew on a rich musical history that stretched back to the time of slavery, and to Africa before that. For centuries, black slaves in the U.S. had harnessed the power of field hollers and work songs that made long days toiling under a hot sun more bearable, and helped a people to remember who they were. Spirituals and hymns were also a safe way to express powerful pent-up emotions like sorrow, anger, and even joy. From these roots came blues music, and later the jazz and bebop that John Coltrane embraced so passionately.

John grew up in his grandfather's church, and in his grandfather's home. With his mother as singer and organist for church services, and his father a talented amateur musician (who sang and played clarinet, guitar, ukulele, and violin), John was surrounded by a love and appreciation of music and sacred song.

But while most religious black people of the time looked upon popular sounds (blues, swing, and jazz) as "Devil's music," John's family was surprisingly open-minded. John and his cousin Mary would turn up the living room radio and listen to hit songs of the day. They also went to hear big swing bands perform live in their town. When a local pastor started a community band for black children, John had the chance to learn an instrument, with free lessons given in his late grandfather's church.

Perhaps more than any other jazz musician, John Coltrane let his religious feelings guide and inspire his work. Of his recovery from drug use, he wrote, "During the year 1957, I experienced, by the grace of God, a spiritual awakening which was to lead me to a richer, fuller, more productive life. At that time, in gratitude, I humbly asked to be given the means and privilege to make others happy through music. I feel this has been granted through His grace."

AUTHOR'S NOTE: Musicians and Drug Use

John Coltrane began drinking alcohol at around age fifteen or sixteen, only a few years after the deaths of his grandfather, father, grandmother, and uncle. When a young person loses a parent or other family members, the effect on his or her life can be profound. John's losses—all within a period of two years—left him burdened with a sadness that followed him throughout his life. Fortunately, he was able to find in music a way to work out many of his emotional struggles. At first a tool to better understand and improve himself, it later became a gift to all who heard him play.

A quiet, thoughtful boy who often felt lonely, John used alcohol to dull the ache of painful or difficult feelings. As a young man and adult, he was on the road performing for weeks or months at a time, where fellow musicians introduced him to drugs like marijuana, cocaine, and heroin. After a while—despite his continued growth as a musician—he began to rely on these substances and found it difficult to stop. Only when his life and career fell apart did he finally choose to remain alcohol- and drug-free.

Musicians are no different from other people who use cigarettes, alcohol, and illegal drugs to deal with fear, anger, sadness, and physical or emotional pain. What makes certain musicians even more vulnerable to the lures of substance use are the demands of touring and performing (stage fright, fatigue, absence from home), the pressure to develop one's talent (self-criticism, financial worries, family responsibilities), and the belief that drugs can somehow make a person more free or creative as an artist.

John Coltrane died at age forty, from liver cancer that may have been related to his early alcohol and drug use. Still, it was his commitment to sobriety, for the last ten years of his life, that allowed him to pursue his spiritual vision and to create some of the most enduring music in the field of jazz.

ARTIST'S NOTE:

I remember being thirteen years old and dreaming of creating album covers, particularly for Mr. Carlos Santana, whose music really affected me and who is someone I would call one of my "artistic angels." His music eventually led me to understand the relationship between spirituality and art. This understanding took me directly to the land of Mr. John Coltrane, who for me is the epitome of these artistic, inspirational angels.

So another dream was born to pay tribute to John Coltrane, and that dream was answered by doing this book. Although I had already been greatly touched and influenced by John Coltrane's music, I found myself digging deeper and really immersing myself in books about him, interviews, and videos of his music. To do the best work I could, I felt I should be as open and receptive as possible. So while working on the art, I decided to fast for two weeks (living on juices and vitamins) while focusing, meditating, praying, and painting. I asked to be used as a vessel and to make the right choices to honor the story of John Coltrane and do justice to the words of Gary Golio. One day during these two weeks, I heard an interview with Alice Coltrane, a great musician in her own right and John's second wife. She spoke about how John had fasted, prayed, and meditated for several days locked up in a room, and when he emerged he had composed the music for his great album *A Love Supreme*. (This music has been a constant presence in my life.) While listening to this interview, I felt an incredible energy come through me that pushed me to the end of the project.

The artwork for this book includes acrylic paintings and some mixed media pieces done with colored pencils, crayons, and acrylics. Many of them started as charcoal drawings that were then layered with paint. Layers really make up a lot of what I do, and these paintings are no exception. I tend to see in terms of layers of reality and layers of spirit, and this makes up my so-called style, which I prefer to call "language."

I've been blessed to see many of my dreams materialize, and I've realized that being true to my path has led me to my dreams. By the way, many years later I did get to do that Santana cover, just as I got to do this book. My art has taken me to many different parts of the world, where I've had the pleasure of seeing and learning many things and meeting many great people. Art has taught me to believe in magic, to believe in dreams. . . . Many artists, like Mr. John Coltrane, have taught me this.

SOURCES AND RESOURCES

BOOKS

Fraim, John. *Spirit Catcher: The Life and Art of John Coltrane*. West Liberty, Ohio: Great House, 1996.

Porter, Lewis. *John Coltrane: His Life and Music*. Ann Arbor: University of Michigan Press, 1998.

Simpkins, C. O. *Coltrane: A Biography*. Baltimore: Black Classic Press, 1989.

Thomas, J. C. *Coltrane: Chasin' the Trane*. New York: Da Capo Press, Inc., 2003.

SELECTED DISCOGRAPHY: CDS AND DVDS

Coltrane, John. *A Love Supreme*. Universal City, Calif.: Impulse Records, distributed by Universal Music & Video Distribution Corp., 2003. CD.

———. *Giant Steps*. Los Angeles: Rhino Records, distributed by Atlantic, 1998. CD.

———. *My Favorite Things*. New York: Atlantic; Los Angeles: Rhino, 1998. CD.

———. *Soultrane*. Berkeley, Calif.: Prestige, 2006. CD.

———. *The Very Best of John Coltrane*. Universal City, Calif.: Impulse Records, distributed by Universal Music & Video Distribution Corp., 2001. CD.

Davis, Miles. *Kind of Blue*. New York: Sony BMG Music Entertainment, distributed by Columbia Records, 2004. CD.

The World According to John Coltrane. BMG, 2002. DVD.

WEBSITE

www.johncoltrane.com The official John Coltrane website, run by the Coltrane family foundation, with extended music selections, a gallery of photographs, and information about scholarships for music students.

Clarion Books • 215 Park Avenue South, New York, New York 10003 • Text copyright © 2012 by Gary Golio • Illustrations copyright © 2012 by Rudy Gutierrez

All rights reserved. • For information about permission to reproduce selections from this book, write to Permissions, Houghton Mifflin Harcourt Publishing Company,

215 Park Avenue South, New York, New York 10003. • Clarion Books is an imprint of Houghton Mifflin Harcourt Publishing Company. • www.hmhbooks.com

The text was set in LA Headlights BTN. • The illustrations were executed in acrylic. • Book design by Sharismar Rodriguez

Library of Congress Cataloging-in-Publication Data • Golio, Gary. • Spirit seeker : John Coltrane's musical journey /

by Gary Golio; paintings by Rudy Gutierrez. • p. cm. • ISBN 978-0-547-23994-1 (hardcover)

1. Coltrane, John, 1926–1967—Juvenile literature. 2. Jazz musicians—

United States—Biography—Juvenile literature. 3. Saxophonists—United States—

Biography—Juvenile literature. I. Gutierrez, Rudy, ill. II. Title.

ML3930.C535G65 2012

788.7'165092—dc23   [B]

2011045948

Manufactured in China

LEO 10 9 8 7 6 5 4 3 2 1

4500371486

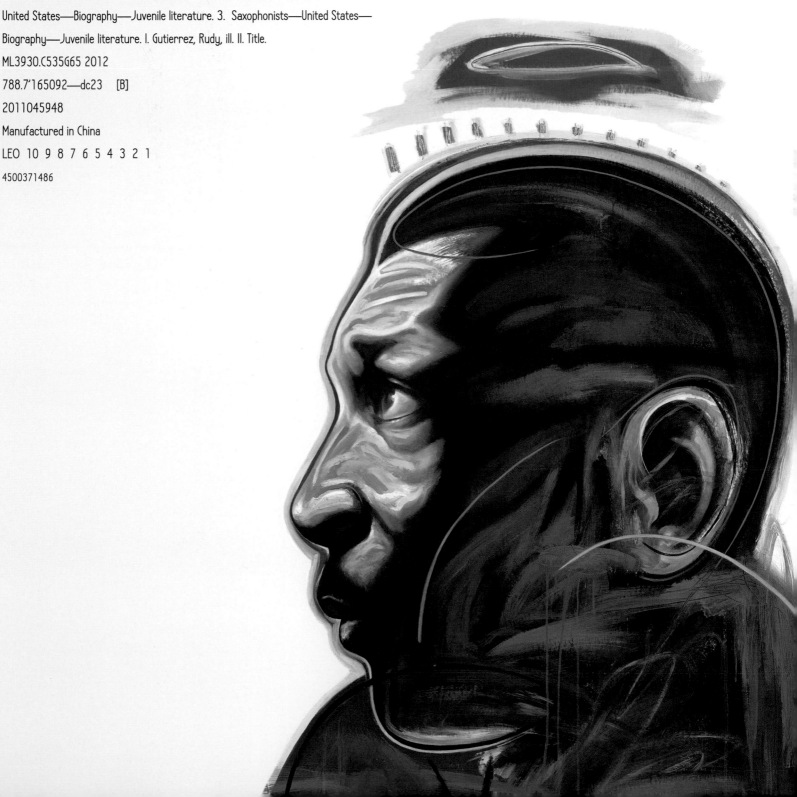